Shirley Barber's
SPELLBOUND
and The Fairy Book

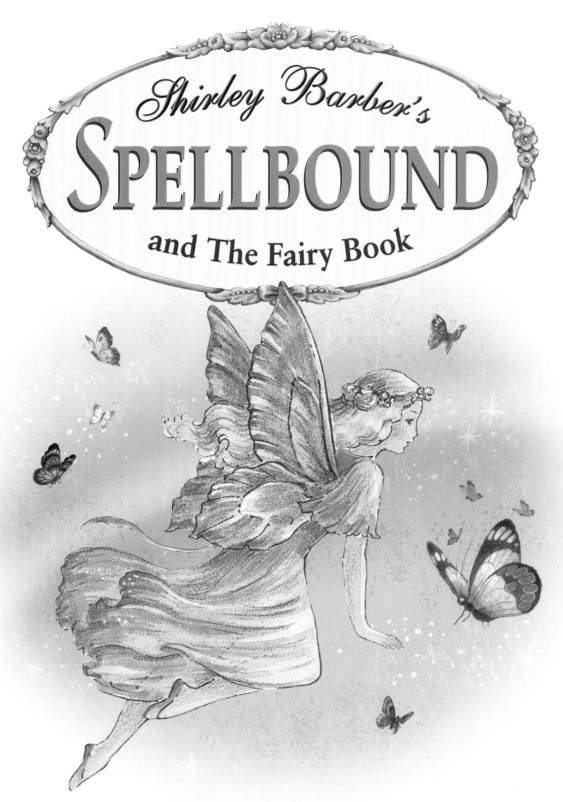

Table of Contents

The Five Mile Press

The Five Mile Press Pty Ltd
950 Stud Road, Rowville
Victoria 3178 Australia
Email: publishing@fivemile.com.au
Website: www.fivemile.com.au

This edition first published 2005

Text and illustrations © Marbit Pty Ltd
www.shirleybarbers.com
CD produced by Spoken Word Productions
This format © The Five Mile Press Pty Ltd
Graphic design by Sonia Dixon

Printed in China

National Library of Australia Cataloguing-in-Publication data

Barber, Shirley.
Shirley Barber's Spellbound and The fairy book.

For children.
ISBN 1 74124 486 2.

I. Barber, Shirley. The fairy book.

A823.3

SPELLBOUND

A Fairytale Romance

$\mathcal{O}$nce upon a time some fairy folk lived in a little town by a sparkling stream. Their tiny houses were built among mossy boulders, half hidden by drooping ferns. The fairy King and Queen lived with their two daughters in a palace made of leaves and petals and with vine-clad balconies overlooking the water.

Princess Rowena was dark-eyed and raven-haired, and little Lisette was the fairest of all the golden fairies. But Princess Lisette was so sweet-natured and so lovely to look upon that Princess Rowena, though equally beautiful, became troubled by envy and deeply unhappy.

The King was kept busy with the affairs of his kingdom, and the Queen by her younger children, so neither noticed their daughter's unhappiness.

$\mathcal{P}$rincess Rowena was some years older
than Princess Lisette, and had helped to care for her as a
child. But as the little golden fairy grew into a beautiful
young girl, so too did the envy grow in her elder sister.

Princess Rowena had found she was able to cast spells,
which was a rare and valued gift among her people. She
knew she should never misuse her gift to harm others,
but gradually her envy overcame her better feelings. She
ordered a golden armlet to be made, and as the jewels
were set in it she imbued it with a powerful spell.

One evening, Rowena gave her sister
the magic armlet. Lisette exclaimed with delight as its
jewels sparkled in the lamplight. "I shall always wear it,
dear Rowena," she promised, as she slid it upon her
arm. "It is so sweet of you, but then, you have always
been such a kind sister to me."

Rowena went to stand for a while on
the balcony and gazed down at the moonlit water. She
knew that while her beautiful sister was bound by the
spell in the armlet she would become tired and unable to
fly as a fairy should. The envy within her was satisfied,
but her heart was heavy for she knew she had
done a great wrong.

$\mathcal{N}$ow, in a neighbouring kingdom, two handsome princes were bidding farewell to their father and mother in an airy palace suspended between pink and white foxglove spires. They were about to set out on a journey to find two fairy brides.

"Choose wisely," commanded King Aven. "They must be of royal blood, and beautiful, if possible, for the sake of our people —"

"— and sweet-natured," put in Queen Bel, "so that I may find it easy to love them."

"Healthy and strong," continued the King, "for they must fly with you and help you to care for the fairy people in your kingdom. Remember, Burnet, this kingdom among the foxgloves shall be yours one day, and you, Trefoil, shall have the meadowsweet realm on the banks of the stream."

The princes flew off, together with several
servants carrying provisions for the journey. Prince Burnet had
heard that two beautiful princesses lived downstream, and a
honeybee told him where to find them.

"They live downstream among the ferns," he buzzed.
"I z-z-zee them when I fly down for a drink of water."

At nightfall, the princes arrived at King Azolla's palace. A fanfare of honeysuckle trumpets announced them.

King Azolla and Queen Bryony welcomed them and introduced their daughters. Young Prince Trefoil had no sooner set eyes upon the golden-haired Princess Lisette than his heart was hers forever, while Prince Burnet fell quickly in love with the raven-haired Rowena.

Later, Prince Burnet said to his brother, "I would look no further for my bride than Princess Rowena except that I feel something is wrong here. There is a strange power in the elder sister and a strange weakness in the other. Perhaps I should look elsewhere for my bride."

"But I have found mine," declared Prince Trefoil. "I shall ask Princess Lisette to be my bride."

The next day, Prince Trefoil found Lisette walking among the violets, and gently asked her to marry him. Lisette hung her golden head sadly. "Alas, dear Prince," she sighed. "I don't know why, but I have become too weak to fly. I cannot be your bride, as I would be unable to work alongside you in your kingdom."

Prince Trefoil stood awhile in serious thought, then came to a decision. "Sweet Princess, you are the only one for me. Tomorrow, I shall tell my parents that I must give up my kingdom. It is true that a prince must marry a princess who is able to fly, but an ordinary fairy may marry his true love, whether she can fly or not!"

Then he flew away to ask her father for her hand in marriage.

$\mathcal{O}$nce he was out of sight,
Princess Lisette shed bitter tears.
"I cannot let my dear Prince ruin his life for me,"
she sobbed. "I shall go far away where he can't find me.
Then perhaps he will forget me and marry
another fairy who can fly."

She walked out over the floating leaves of
water plants and stepped into a fallen leaf. She pushed
it into the middle of the stream where the fast-flowing
current carried her swiftly down the valley.

15

Meanwhile, King Azolla and the two princes
spent much time in anxious talk. The King praised
Trefoil for the strength of his love, but said he must
not give up his kingdom without consulting his
parents.

Suddenly, word came that Princess Lisette was
missing. They all joined in the search for her, but she
was nowhere to be found.

After several days of searching, all hope of finding her
was gone, but the heart-broken Prince Trefoil
announced he would keep looking until he found her.
Nothing his brother or the King and Queen said could
make him change his mind, and he flew
away alone, down the valley into
wild regions where no fairies
had ventured before.

17

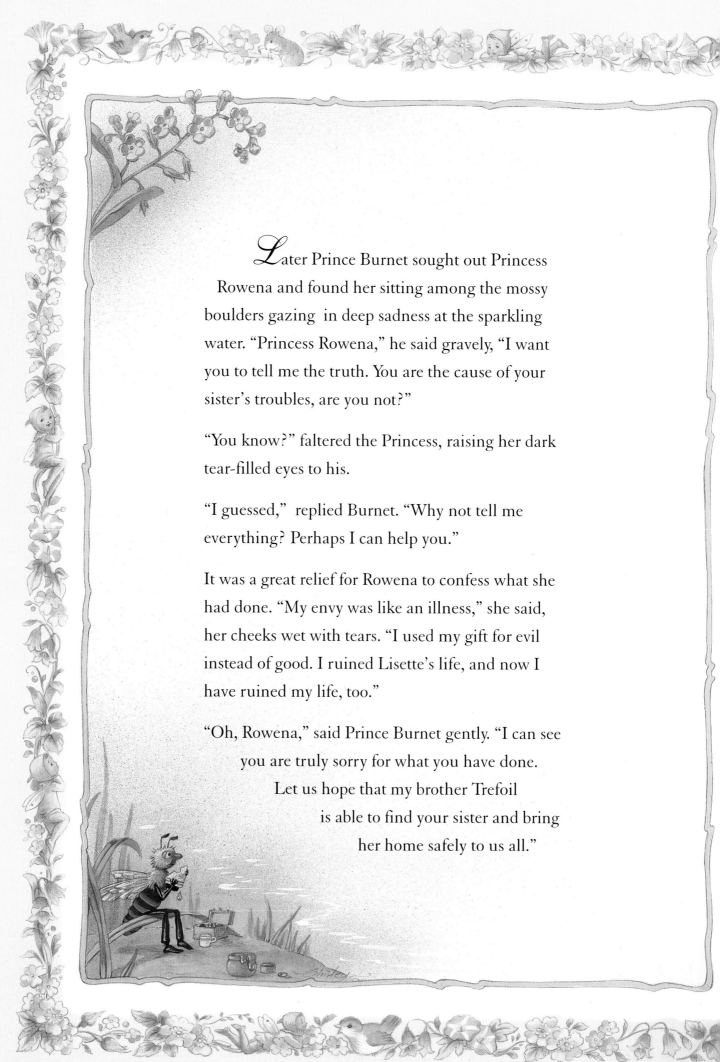

$\mathcal{L}$ater Prince Burnet sought out Princess Rowena and found her sitting among the mossy boulders gazing in deep sadness at the sparkling water. "Princess Rowena," he said gravely, "I want you to tell me the truth. You are the cause of your sister's troubles, are you not?"

"You know?" faltered the Princess, raising her dark tear-filled eyes to his.

"I guessed," replied Burnet. "Why not tell me everything? Perhaps I can help you."

It was a great relief for Rowena to confess what she had done. "My envy was like an illness," she said, her cheeks wet with tears. "I used my gift for evil instead of good. I ruined Lisette's life, and now I have ruined my life, too."

"Oh, Rowena," said Prince Burnet gently. "I can see you are truly sorry for what you have done. Let us hope that my brother Trefoil is able to find your sister and bring her home safely to us all."

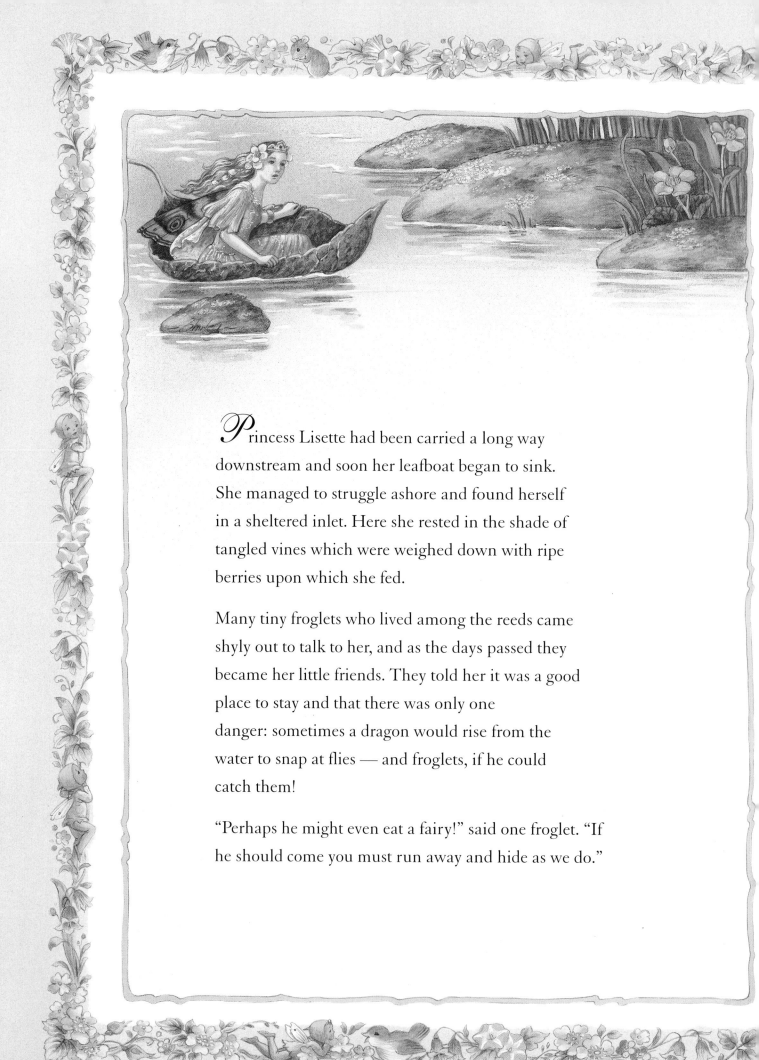

$\mathcal{P}$rincess Lisette had been carried a long way downstream and soon her leafboat began to sink. She managed to struggle ashore and found herself in a sheltered inlet. Here she rested in the shade of tangled vines which were weighed down with ripe berries upon which she fed.

Many tiny froglets who lived among the reeds came shyly out to talk to her, and as the days passed they became her little friends. They told her it was a good place to stay and that there was only one danger: sometimes a dragon would rise from the water to snap at flies — and froglets, if he could catch them!

"Perhaps he might even eat a fairy!" said one froglet. "If he should come you must run away and hide as we do."

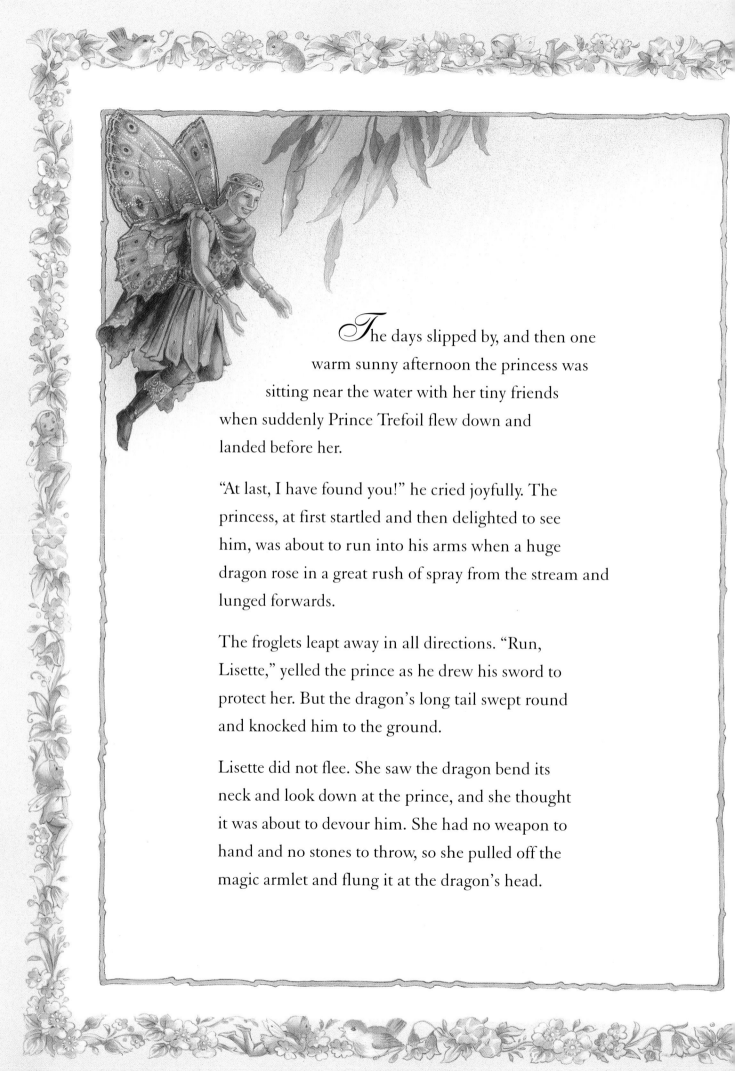

The days slipped by, and then one warm sunny afternoon the princess was sitting near the water with her tiny friends when suddenly Prince Trefoil flew down and landed before her.

"At last, I have found you!" he cried joyfully. The princess, at first startled and then delighted to see him, was about to run into his arms when a huge dragon rose in a great rush of spray from the stream and lunged forwards.

The froglets leapt away in all directions. "Run, Lisette," yelled the prince as he drew his sword to protect her. But the dragon's long tail swept round and knocked him to the ground.

Lisette did not flee. She saw the dragon bend its neck and look down at the prince, and she thought it was about to devour him. She had no weapon to hand and no stones to throw, so she pulled off the magic armlet and flung it at the dragon's head.

The spinning armlet flashed in the sunlight,
and the dragon snapped at it and swallowed it whole. Then,
its magic spell began to work, and sapped him of his strength.
He fell back into the stream and sank slowly into its depths,
never to return.

$\mathcal{T}$he dragon's claw had wounded Prince Trefoil, but Princess Lisette made bandages of cobwebs and healing salves from streamside herbs. As he regained his strength, so too did she recover hers and she soon found that she could fly once more. At last, the day came for them to say goodbye to their froglet friends, and together they flew up the valley to the fern kingdom of King Azolla.

What cheers and rejoicing took place when they arrived! A huge feast was prepared to welcome them, and there it was announced that Princess Rowena would marry Prince Burnet, while Princess Lisette would marry her beloved Trefoil. In a moment of quiet, Rowena spoke sorrowfully to her sister of her wrong-doing, and begged for her forgiveness. Lisette lovingly forgave her, and together the two couples planned happily for their wedding.

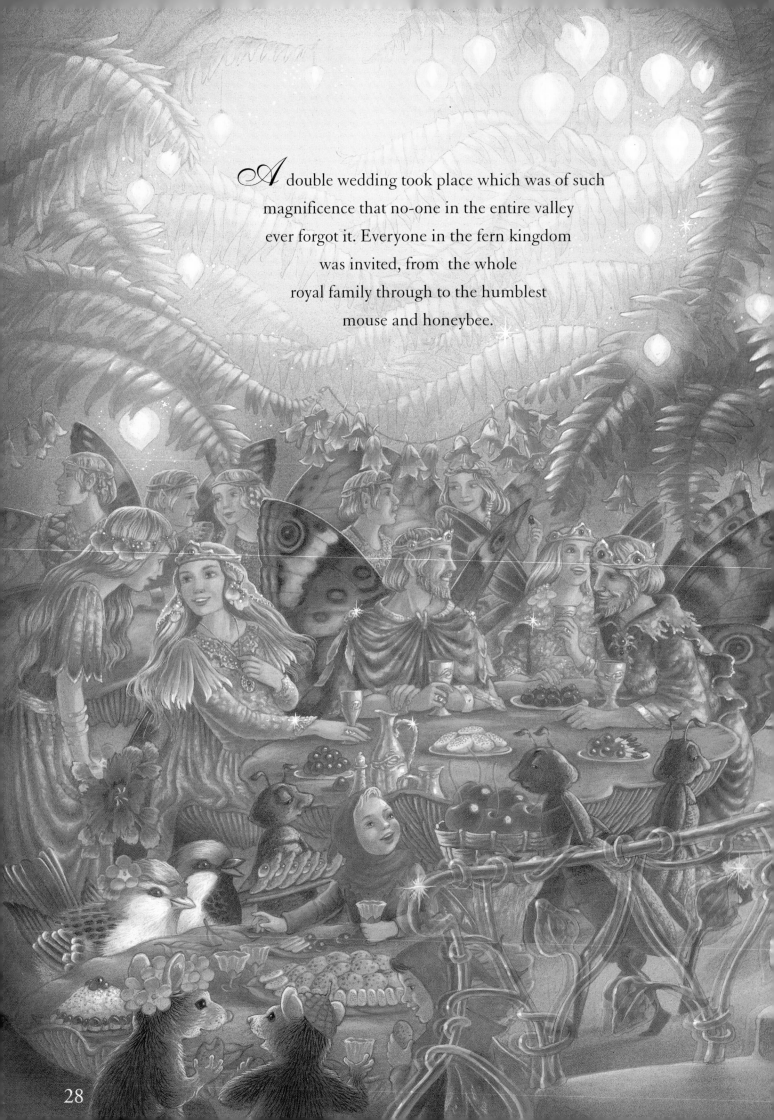

A double wedding took place which was of such
magnificence that no-one in the entire valley
ever forgot it. Everyone in the fern kingdom
was invited, from the whole
royal family through to the humblest
mouse and honeybee.

*T*he happy fairy couples flew
away to their new homes among
the foxgloves and meadowsweet.

Princess Rowena only used her gift
for the good of others — so the fairy folk
lived happily ever after.

And the dragon who had swallowed the armlet
lay spellbound at the bottom of the stream, never to
frighten the froglets again.

THE FAIRY BOOK

An Anthology of Verse

The Fairy's Tree

I've never seen a fairy
But I know just where she'd hide.
I'm sure I've found her hollow tree
'Cos when I peep inside
I see a cobweb cover,
Moss pillow for her head,
A little glow-worm night-light,
(I think she reads in bed!)
There's her toadstool table,
And on it I can see
A gumnut cup and saucer
For her morning cup of tea.
I think the fairy's hiding
In the shadows out of sight.
I'll go back home to dinner now
And to her I will write
A teeny-weeny letter
And this is what I'll say:—
"I'd love to meet you, Fairy,
Will you please come out and play!"

Shirley Barber

Toadstools

It's not a bit windy,
It's not a bit wet,
The sky is as sunny
As summer, and yet
Little umbrellas are
Everywhere spread,
Pink ones, and brown ones,
And orange, and red.

I can't see the folks
Who are hidden below;
I've peeped, and I've peeped
Round the edges but no!
They hold their umbrellas
So tight and so close
That nothing shows under,
Not even a nose!

Elizabeth Fleming

Elfland Horns

The splendour falls on castle walls
And snowy summits old in story:
The long light shakes across the lakes,
And the wild cataract leaps in glory.
Blow, bugle, blow, set the wild echoes flying,
Blow, bugle; answer echoes, dying, dying, dying.

O hark, O hear! how thin and clear,
And thinner, clearer, farther going!
O sweet and far from cliff and scar
The horns of Elfland faintly blowing!
Blow, bugle, blow, set the wild echoes flying,
Blow, bugle; answer echoes, dying, dying, dying.

Alfred, Lord Tennyson

The Fairies

Up the airy mountain,
　　Down the rushy glen,
We daren't go a-hunting
　　For fear of little men.
Wee folk, good folk,
　　Trooping all together;
Green jacket, red cap,
　　And white owl's feather!

Down along the rocky shore
　　Some make their home.
They live on crispy pancakes
　　Of yellow tide-foam;
Some in the reeds
　　Of the black mountain lake,
With frogs for their watchdogs,
　　All night awake.

William Allingham

Bedtime Story

Tell me my favourite story
While I am snuggling down,
About the beautiful fairy
Who wears a sparkling gown.

Tell me about her silken hair,
Her rainbow-coloured wings.
Tell of her bag of magic stars;
Sing me the song she sings.

Tell me she flies through the forest dark
And after a while she hears
A poor little bunny crying,
So, gently she dries his tears.

She carries him home to his burrow
So he's just in time for tea.
(His mother was looking out for him
Just as you look for me!)

For an hour or so she lingers.
She sings the bunny to sleep,
Then leaves behind on his pillow
A magical star to keep.

I'll help you remember the wording.
It has to be told just right.
And then you can tell me it all again
Tomorrow — and every night!

Shirley Barber

36

The Flowers

All the names I know from nurse:
Gardener's Garters, Shepherd's Purse;
Bachelor's Buttons, Lady's Smock,
And the Lady Hollyhock.

Fairy places, fairy things,
Fairy woods where the wild bee wings,
Tiny trees for tiny dames —
These must all be fairy names!

Tiny woods below whose boughs
Shady fairies weave a house;
Tiny treetops, rose or thyme,
Where the braver fairies climb!

Fair are grown up people's trees,
But the fairest woods are these;
Where, if I were not so tall,
I should live for good and all.

Robert Louis Stevenson

The Miniature World

If I was very, very small
The jointed grasses would be tall,
And I would climb up them like trees
To wave to passing honey bees.
And then I think I'd like to try
To ride a big blue dragon-fly —
Zigzag around the sky like mad
Then land it on a lily-pad.
When I was hungry I would eat
Sorrel, mint and meadow-sweet.
Maybe I'd leapfrog real frogs,
Or maybe dive off mossy logs
Into pools deep, cool and dim,
And with the little tadpoles swim.
Of course, it would be very scary
Meeting spiders, black and hairy!
And those giant drops of dew —
I guess I'd have to dodge them too!
But it would be so nice to know
The hidden paths where Fairies go,
And oh! so good to spend my days
Exploring, secret forest ways...
And when I was too tired to roam
I'd hail a beetle and ride home!

Shirley Barber

The Fairies' Ball

Katie has a fine doll's house,
 It stands against the wall;
  Her grandma gave it to her and
  It's elegant and tall.

 Katie said, at midnight,
  Or perhaps a little after,
   She was woken by the tiny sounds
   Of music and of laughter.

  She sat up in her bed and thought
   She really must be dreaming —
    From every little doll's house window
    Golden light was streaming.

She crept across to see what could
Be going on in there,
And saw it was a fairies' ball —
A very grand affair.

All night the fairies revelled, then
At dawn, away they flew.
Now Katie's just a little cross
At all there is to do.

She doesn't mind her doll's house used
By fairies and by elves,
But thinks that they should always
Clean up afterwards themselves!

Shirley Barber

The Fairy Market

My grandma, when a little child,
One silver moonlit night,
Climbed up the hill behind her home
And saw a magic sight;
Among the tangled rowan trees
Within a ferny dell,
A crowd of fairy folk had come
Their goods to buy and sell.
Bright lanterns lit the market stalls
Whereon lay lovely things,
Gleaming wands and cobweb shawls,
Necklaces and rings;
Elfin caps and buckled shoes,
Berries, fruit and bread —
"And then I saw this silver chain
And loved it," Grandma said.
"So out I bravely stepped and went
Into the fairy throng.
"I bought the chain — will you believe? —
It only cost a song!"

Shirley Barber

42

The Rainbow Stairway

The lightning made us jump,
The thunder was much too loud,
The rain came down in a torrent,
But now, against the cloud,
The garden glows in the sunlight;
We stare at the golden hill. For look!
Through the sparkling raindrops,
Which gently shower still,
There's a rainbow stairway curving
Down from the sky's grey-blue,
So fairies can climb to their ballroom —
Shall we run and climb it too?

Shirley Barber

The Fairy Swing

Down in the apple orchard
White petals fell like rain
Round little Mary Catherine
As she made a daisy-chain.

She used a lot of daisies,
She fashioned it with care —
Heard her mother calling her,
And left it hanging there.

When later she went back again
She heard a wee voice singing,
And in her daisy-chain she saw
A lovely fairy swinging.

Now, Mary Catherine always leaves
Her daisy-chains behind.
If fairies use them for their swings
She says she doesn't mind.

Shirley Barber

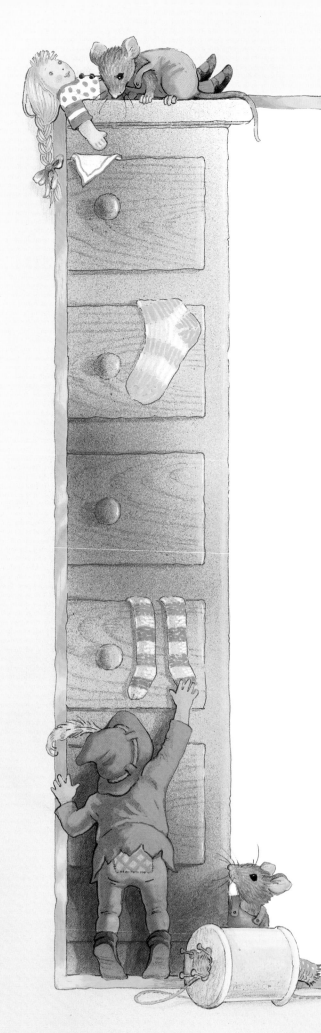

Elfin Friends

Uncle William knew an elf,
"A manikin," he said,
"In pointed hat and buckled shoes
And a suit of green and red."

Aunt Betty knew an elf
Of whom she grew quite fond.
They quarrelled when he tried to fish
The goldfish from her pond.

My grandma said a little elf
She often used to see.
He'd visit her to chat and drink
A thimbleful of tea.

She knitted him a woolly cap
With flaps to warm his ears,
And he was very grateful —
They were friends for years and years.

They teach you really silly things
When first you go to school,
Like knitting useless woolly snakes
Right through a wooden spool.

But I had such a good idea —
In red and green and white
I've knitted socks for chilly elves,
(I hope they're not *too* bright!)

If I can stay awake tonight,
And if there is an elf,
And if he likes his socks, I'll have
An elfin friend myself.

Shirley Barber

The Little Elfman

I met a little elfman once,
Down where the lilies blow.
I asked him why he was so small.
And why he didn't grow.

He slightly frowned, and with his eye
He looked me through and through —
"I'm just as big for me," said he,
"As you are big for you!"

John Kendrick Bangs

The Tea Party

A robin brought the message —
She'll come at half-past three.
We'll sit where it is shady
Beneath the willow tree.
I'll make some tiny sandwiches,
Fill flower cups with dew.
A pollen cake I'll try to make
And daisy biscuits too.
I'll lay upon this toadstool
Rose petal plates for three.
The table must look pretty when
A Fairy comes to tea.

Shirley Barber

47

The Fairy Queen

The woodland is hushed —
It seems to be waiting.
Even the breeze doesn't stir.
Everything seems to be anticipating
A wonderful thing to occur.
Through bluebells and ferns
A green pathway is wending;
Rabbits each side of it sit.
Above them the blossom boughs
Downward are bending
Where small birds excitedly flit.
Hark! there's the sound of a
Small drummer drumming.
Rabbits respectfully stand.
Now, down the pathway
They're coming! They're coming!
A colourful miniature band!
The mice shake the bluebells
And they begin ringing —
The tiniest tinkling sound.
Now come the baby elves
Hopping and springing
Over the soft mossy ground.
And here are the fairies,
(Oh, can I be dreaming?) —
Some flying, some dancing along.
In jewel-bright garments
Aglitter and gleaming,
They sing such a haunting sweet song.
And lastly, the fairest,
Her delicate dress is
Oh, shimmering gold and pale green;
A diamond crown on her
Floating silk tresses —
The beautiful Fairy Queen!

Shirley Barber

Fairy Dresses

The other day I woke at dawn,
And tiptoed out onto the lawn,
Then I stared in such surprise
At the sight which met my eyes.
Everywhere I looked there were
Veils of jewelled gossamer.
Where the hollyhocks grow tall
Fairy shawls lay over all;
On the rose-arch, in each space,
Petticoats of finest lace.
On the lupins and the phlox
Hung the daintiest fairy frocks,
Diamond-sprinkled, shimmering,
And, in shadows glimmering,
Sequinned cloaks for evening wear;
Twinkling strands for golden hair.
Someone, (hiding I suppose),
Must have fashioned all those clothes,
Hoped a fairy passing by
Would fly down her dress to buy.
But — whose fingers, small but strong
Had been so busy all night long?

Shirley Barber

50

Fairy-wear

A Cowslip flower will make a hat
   for any little elf;
With Pennywort umbrellas he
   can always shade himself.
Wild Arum makes both hood and cape
   if it should start to rain,
At night a Lamb's Ear leaf can be
   his furry counterpane.

In the hedge, Convolvulus
   has flowers light and airy;
Neatly pleated flaring dresses
   fit for any fairy.
A spangled wrap of lacy webs
   draped softly over all,
A crown of Hawthorn buds and she
   is ready for the ball.

Shirley Barber

51

Water Babies

Where do the Water Babies dwell —
Does anyone know, can anyone tell?
"Yes," said a mermaid sweet to me,
"They live beside the bright blue sea."

"Down on the sands they come and play,
They paddle in the sea all day;
With tiny dimpled naked feet,
I've seen them!" cried a mermaid sweet.

And she was right — I've seen them too,
Little white feet in the water blue;
Scampering merrily hand in hand,
All along the golden sand.

No wonder the sea laughs all day long.
And sings them such a happy song;
I've seen them there, so I know well,
That's where the Water Babies dwell.

Unknown

The Mermaid's Child

Down by the sea Louisa found
A mermaid's baby (so she said).
It lay within an ormer shell,
Curled up as if that was its bed.

She fed it sea-foam cake and when
It cried she gave its face a kiss.
She combed its curls, and cuddled it —
Oh! we got very tired of this!

She wouldn't swim or play with us
She stayed beside it all the day.
Thank goodness when the tide came in
The mermaids took their child away.

Shirley Barber

The Dream Fairy

A little fairy comes at night,
Her eyes are blue, her hair is brown,
With silver spots upon her wings,
And from the moon she flutters down.

She has a little silver wand,
And when a good child goes to bed
She waves her wand from right to left
And makes a circle round her head.

And then it dreams of pleasant things,
Of fountains filled with fairy fish,
And trees that bear delicious fruit,
And bow their branches at a wish;

Of arbors filled with dainty scents
From lovely flowers that never fade,
Bright 'flies that flitter in the sun,
And glow-worms shining in the shade;

And talking birds with gifted tongues
For singing songs and telling tales,
And pretty dwarfs to show the way
Through the fairy hills and fairy dales.

Thomas Hood

54

The Fairy Folk

Come cuddle close in Daddy's coat
Beside the fire so bright,
And hear about the fairy folk
That wander in the night.
For when the stars are shining clear
And all the world is still,
They float across the silver moon
From hill to cloudy hill.

Their caps of red, their cloaks of green,
Are hung with silver bells,
And when they're shaken with the wind
Their merry ringing swells.
And riding on the crimson moth,
With black spots on her wings,
They guide them down the purple sky
With golden bridle rings.

They love to visit girls and boys
To see how sweet they sleep,
To stand beside their cosy cots
And at their faces peep.
For in the whole of Fairyland
They have no finer sight
Than little children sleeping sound
With faces rosy bright.

Robert M. Bird

The Fairy Book

In summer, when the grass is thick,
   if Mother has the time,
She shows me with her pencil how
   a poet makes a rhyme,
And often she is sweet enough
   to choose a leafy nook,
Where I cuddle up so closely
   when she reads the Fairy book.

In winter, when the corn's asleep,
   and birds are not in song,
And crocuses and violets have
   been away too long,
Dear mother puts her thimble by
   in an answer to my look,
And I cuddle up so closely when
   she reads the Fairy book.

Norman Gale

The Little Folk

In Spring, when the cherry-plum blossom
Lay soft as pink foam in the trees,
I saw them descend on the garden.
At first, sure, I thought it was bees!

Down where the petals were scattered,
Laughing and singing they came.
I watched from my window astonished —
The Little Folk playing a game.

They swung from the flower-laden branches.
They twisted and spun on the wing.
Their singing was sweeter than silver
As they sang and they danced in a ring.

Well! I never saw a sight like it —
The Little Folk all at their play.
Then Pussy ran out from the bushes,
And up they all flew — and away!

Shirley Barber

Midnight Fishing

The crescent moon is riding high
Like a silver ship in the midnight sky.
Those misty veils
Are silken sails
And we can go fishing, you and I.

We'll rock on waves of deepest blue.
We'll cast our nets like the sailors do.
Each shining fish
Is a tiny wish,
And we'll make sure to bring home a few.

We'll moor by a cloud in Scorpio.
You're much braver than I am, so
Lean out and grab
A spangled crab
While I drop my line in the depths below.

We're sailing home by dawn's pink light.
With a glittering crab and the wishes bright,
The silvery gleam
Of a fisherman's dream —
Oh! let's go fishing again tonight.

Shirley Barber

Twelve O'clock — Fairy-time

Through the house give glimmering light
By the dead and drowsy fire;
Every elf and fairy sprite
Hop as light as bird from brier.

. . . .

Now, until the break of day,
Through this house each fairy stray.

William Shakespeare